Against His Will

A Novelette

Simernecia Shena

Will is a work of fiction. Any references or similarities to actual events, real people, living or dead, or to real locales are intended to give the novel a sense of reality. Any similarity in other names, characters, places and incidents is entirely coincidental.

ISBN: 9781092529143

Acknowledgments

Let me start by saying that there is a tremendous amount of power in the word prayer! God, I am forever grateful for every single avenue you have placed me on and guided me along the way. Without you I am nothing, your work is amazing, and your promises are real. I will praise you every day of my life because you are worthy. To my children, I fight vigorously because of you, I feel as though I must do everything in my power to keep you girls proud. Shay, you give me strength and courage, you are my teacher, my cheerleader, and often my headache, I love you beyond the stars.

Toodie, you came along and brought my growth and my strive for building my own independence. I love you both so much and wouldn't trade you for the universe. It is so many people I would like to thank for their own personal reasons, but it's too many to name. Please know that I see your support and I'm grateful and humble, God has placed an overwhelming amount of great people in my life and I love each of you. To my readers, I will always appreciate you for allowing me and my work into your minds, thank you, thank you, thank you.

Simernecia Shena

Against His will

Against His Will

Against His will

6

Interlude

2006

"Paw Paw Mackie, Niko should want to do something more productive with his life instead of being at this shop 24/7 and you should encourage him to." Ashaunti whined to her grandfather.

"Ashaunti, I keep the kids what more do you want from me? Nothing I do is good enough, it's like you want me to be in the streets are something." I explained.

"Now listen baby girl, Niko is there for you when you need him to be, Ashaunti you must learn to be there for him too, marriage is a team effort, I don't care how young you are. Now tell me what's wrong with him being down here at the shop trying to learn something? Niko is a good young man he's going to get better, but you can't give up on him." Paw Paw Mackie chimed in patting me on my shoulders.

"The two of you promise me one thing promise me that whatever your marriage withstands, you will find a way of reasoning and work it out. If I leave this world, I'm leaving everything behind for you two and those children, so I would advise you both to figure

out how to compromise." Paw Paw Mackie said

pointing at Ashaunti and myself.

Niko

Present Day

"Niko, how long do you plan on sleeping today? I have more than enough to take care of this morning. It would be nice if you made sure the twin's got to school. Nila has a mandatory conference today, I don't know why she decided to wait until the end of senior year to start acting out. Both Nila and Niko Jr. have testing today, I have a hair appointment scheduled for today it would be nice if you could handle your own children this one time. Niko! I know you hear me talking to you a simple okay would be fine." Ashaunti woke up this morning in rare form.

"Alright."

"Why do I consistently tolerate this from you? I just know life is better somewhere else. Niko you have terrible work habits, all you ever do is hang at the damn mechanic shop, working on your own motorcycle. How is that supposed to bring steady income into this household?"

I laid there and listening to her go on and on, intaking every word she released from her mouth. My mind wanted to retaliate however, that would on matters worse and it's too early in the morning to be arguing with my wife.

"Ashaunti, I hear you now will you please stop before the twin's think we're into it or something."

"Niko when did you start thinking about how the kids feel? I wonder how the kids feel about your job or the fact that you are hardly around. You spend every bit of your time at that shop, you're never spending time with your children. But you care how they feel and what they hear, you barely work on cars just over there playing with that motorbike, Niko we need real money and you sir need a real job."

Knock Knock Ashaunti was interrupted by the knock on the door.

"Can I come in?" Nila our teenage daughter asked.

"What do you need Nila?" Ashaunti answered.

"Who is bring me and Niko Jr. to school, we're already running late?"

"I am baby girl I'll be out shortly, give daddy a minute." I answered her getting out of bed staring at Ashaunti.

Ashaunti was now fully dressed and look like she just had her hair done. Although I didn't mention it to her, she wore some skin tight jeans, with a top on that had her stomach exposed, my wife was looking good.

"Ashaunti, why does Nila have a conference today, what's going on with her?" I was confused because Nila is typically our good kid.

"Niko, apparently Nila has been reaching for attention and I can't tell you why. Her counselor stated that she has been acting out with her attitude and behavior. This is her senior year and the wrong time for her to begin acting out, you know that."

"Ashaunti, maybe you should attend this meeting as well," I mentioned walking out of the bathroom grabbing my Ralph Lauren joggers.

"I told you why I could not make it, you can handle something's occasionally, it is not like you do anything else. Niko you uphold those children with everything that they do so now you can see first hand! Niko Jr. walks in this house every night smelling like marijuana, with blood shot eyes, high as giraffe pussy. Your son has failing grades, I fuss, fuss, cuss, and fuss some more I should not have to do all of that. Nila don't get me started on her, she always has the phone in her hands, and always in some mess with other girls over some pissy ass lil boy. We were supposed to be a team; however, I feel like I should have been a single mother." Ashaunti threw her hands up in an irritated way and walked off.

There was nothing else I could say, aside from Ashaunti's constant nagging our marriage was ice cold, we were both unhappy. Me and my wife have been together forever, I don't know anything else besides my wife, and it's the same for her.

When Ashaunti became pregnant in high school her mother's first words were, "Ain't no daughter of mine having a baby out of wedlock!" My mother in law meant those words, at seventeen years old me and Ashaunti were at the courthouse getting married. My mother had similar views however, she was a little hood. "Niko, if you wanna be a man, you damn well going to do what a man should do. I'm not raising nobody else's baby are in your case babies, go on ahead and marry that girl."

Neither one of us were prepared for a marriage or babies, but it happened and almost seventeen years later here we are. It was not an ideal situation, but it hasn't been the worse either. About six years into our marriage,

Ashaunti's grandfather passed away, he left behind a house and his prized possession, his mechanic shop, both of which was inherited by my wife and myself. Ashaunti comes from a family that was more financially stable then where I come from, they spoiled her. When I became her husband, I could not offer her half of what she was accustomed to. I tried and I tried hard to do it, after some time I gave up. When we both finished high school, Ashaunti went off to pursue nursing school while I cared for the twins. That's how I grew to love the mechanic shop, Paw Paw Mackie would tell me, "Bring the kids with you and come give me a hand at the shop." Mackie taught me

everything I know about cars, motorcycles, and

trucks. I learned how to repair them, rebuild

and replace them. I can take an entire motor

apart and put it back together. Mackie and I

had our own father-son type of relationship he

would say "Take care of my grandkids or I am

going to take care of you young buck." That old

man was wild, but his words still stick with to

this day.

Me, Nila, and Niko Jr. made it to the school

right after breakfast and class had already

begun.

"Now before we go inside of this school can you tell me what do you have going on Nila? School is for learning however, I hear you have been showing out. What's good, talk to daddy?"

"There isn't anything going on daddy." Nila gazed out of the window.

"Aht, Aht, Aht, stop that lying girl." Niko Jr. said from the backseat.

"Boy if you don't hush up, that is your problem minding business that does not belong to you." Nila said.

"You are my business, ain't that right pops?"

Niko Jr. said with confidence while him and Nila

look at me for my response.

"First off Nila you don't have no business

secondly Niko yes and no."

"Daddy what you mean yes and no?" Nila

interrupted me.

"You're his business when you're at school

acting out and vice versa. Say Niko why is your

mother telling me you coming inside of my

house smelling like weed? You better not be

smoking boy."

"Don't you smoke? But I don't smoke, I be cutting grass that's why sometimes I smell like that." Niko Jr. lied.

"Son, I'm a grown ass man, I can do whatever the hell I want." I said looking at him with a straight face.

"Yeah, you're grown, but aren't you supposed to lead by example?" Nila asked.

"Yes, do as I say and not as I do, that's my example. Now come on let's go inside this school and see what y'all have been up to. Your mother seems to think I can't handle my own children, Nila and Niko y'all better straighten up, and fast." I said.

All three of us walked inside the school, Niko

shot off and went to class, while Nila and I

checked into the office. When we entered all

the ladies were standing around chatting and

laughing.

"Good Morning, may I help you oh I see

you're here checking in." The older lady said

pulling out her ink pen.

"We have a conference with Ms. Labo." Nila

mentioned.

"Oh okay, please have a seat, I will let Ms.

Labo know you're here."

We took a seat and waited, Nila didn't say

much and I wish I knew what was going on

inside of her mind. My baby girl is a beautiful young lady, but Nila has her mother ways Ashaunti would say she has my ways though. It's probably partly my fault because I was never hard on her, Nila has never been a problem however, that Niko Jr. is a character I would expect to be sitting here with him and not his sister.

"Mrs. Alexander, you can send the parents to my office." The voice came through the speaker phone.

"Ms. Labo is ready for you all."

I followed Nila into the office and Ms. Labo looks very familiar.

"Hello Mr. Webb, how are you?" She said

with a welcoming smile.

The shop! That's where I know her from, I

change her oil from time to time.

"Ms. Labo, I would be better if I knew what

was going on with my daughter."

"Well Nila is a great kid she honestly is

however, lately she has been having issues with

authority and controlling her attitude.

Everyone is aware that calculus is very

important course and being disruptive in that

class or any class is not tolerated." She

explained.

"Did her teachers say exactly what was going on?"

Ms. Labo glanced down at some papers in front of her I assumed to be notes.

"Yes, Nila hasn't been completing or turning in assignments and when asked about the work, she creates a scene in front of the class, interrupting other students. Mr. Webb that behavior is unacceptable, the last time Nila was suspended."

"Suspended?"

"Yes, suspended." She replied looking at Nila.

"Mom knows Daddy." Nila said.

"Well I didn't, as you can see Ms. Labo my daughter and wife didn't inform me of this."

"Daddy do you really care?" Nila whipping away her tears.

"Nila don't ask me that, come on Nila you know better, you're trying to flip this around."

"It seems like there are some things going on at home and normally that is where it starts." Ms. Labo input her thoughts.

"Please don't take this as if I am being rude, but I know how to raise my child. I think I have gathered enough information to handle this at home and I assure you she will not be back in your office, right Nila?"

"Right daddy."

"Well that is all if I should need you or Mrs. Webb again, I will give you a call." She ended our meeting.

"Nila have a good day, I will talk to you when you get home." I hugged my daughter and left.

Ashaunti

Niko: Hey Shaunti why didn't you tell me about Nila's suspension?
Me: It slipped my mind, what did the counselor say?
Niko: We will talk about it when I get home.
Me: I'll be in late.

Falling in love young was hard and It was even harder when you had to learn to grow together, my marriage has been on an emotional rollercoaster lately. Yes, my husband stood by my side when I went to school, he even married me when my family asked him to, we were having babies so it was only right. I thought me and Niko would be together forever, but times have changed. I love my husband however, I'm not in love with my husband, in all honesty, I feel like our marriage is coming to an end it's sad to say, but it is the reality. Niko has been needing a real job I'm tired of pulling all the weight around the house by myself, I might as well be by myself. The Bible says a man that doesn't work don't eat the main meal Niko has been missing is pussy.

Niko is not about to eat have a taste and he's not coming home from a real job. Repairing cars and building motorcycles for fun is not bringing bread to the table. That leads me to what I'm about to say next, I must ensure both of our kids have the proper college funding because it is damn sure not coming from the mechanic shop.

I have been seeing someone for a while and he makes it happen! The money he gives me I placed in a special account away for my children. Doc my Doc haha, I met Dr. Fitzgerald on the job, he is the owner of the clinic where I'm employed, his clinic. Doc and I been sexing each other up for a while, but we started to

become sloppy having sex at work, in every

part of that clinic, from the mail room, to the

supply room, even on lunch break fucking all in

the car, wherever he wanted it at, I was ready.

It was great spontaneous sex too however, we

have a new spot now, the Marriott hotel off

Corporate Boulevard. Doc books us a room

once a week on the presidential floor, so I can

fuck him with the window curtains ajar,

overlooking the city of Baton Rouge. It feels

great feeling like you're having sex on top of

the city, I told my husband I had an

appointment and I did, to get fucked like a dog.

I walked into the hotel and straight to the desk.

"Yes, do you have a key for Ashaunti Webb?" I asked the front desk attendant.

"Hello Mrs. Webb, I sure do room 6012 have a nice stay here at the Marriott on Corporate."

"Thank you!" I tipped her and got on the elevator.

I was all wrapped up in a black trench coat with nothing underneath, nothing! As I entered the hotel room, I hear the shower water running, I didn't waste any time opening the curtains, dropping my coat, and laying across the king size bed with my legs spread wide open. A few seconds later I heard the

bathroom door slide open and Doc walked in.

"Are you hungry? I have something for you

to snack on." I said seductively.

"DAMN!!! Like that?" He asked with his fully

erect dick bouncing up and down.

"Come here Doc." I swayed him towards me

and he obeyed.

Doc loves controlling sex he came straight to

me and went to work kissing all over me, but I

wanted something new I wanted to be in

control, so I stopped him.

"Wait stop."

Doc looked at me as if I was disturbing his favorite meal and I knew that I was. He turned over on his back and I sat directly in his face, I started riding the hell out of his face, almost smothering him. I can feel his tongue going in and out of my hole, I grind my hips back and forth I wanted to feel his tongue good and I did too.

"Damn Doc, you're eating me really good. You must have been hungry baby, you been skipping meals? Awwwww." I moaned with my eyes closed in pure pleasure mode.

"Ummm hmm." Was all he could say with a mouth full of me.

"Awwww Doc, I want you to fuck me like a

dog bitch."

I tried to pull my body up, but he pulled me

back down, damn he really is hungry.

"Stay still Ashaunti." Doc said and went back

to eating.

Okay have your way, I could get used to only

getting my pussy ate out. After he was finished,

I rode his dick backwards cowgirl style, when

we both hit a climax, he got dressed to leave.

What I desired more than anything was for Doc

to leave his wife and build a family with me,

that is what I wanted. I decided to take this

moment to tell him how I feel, how long does

he expect me to sleep with him from hotel to hotel. The sex is awesome, but is that all we're doing casual sex here and there?

"Doc when are we going to take the next step?"

"What next step Ashaunti? Where are we stepping to?"

"Really Doc? A relationship, when will we have a solid relationship, you and me?" I rolled my eyes because he was pushing it.

"Ashaunti, why can't you just enjoy these moments without labels and strings being attached? I thought we were enjoying each other's company, you're a married woman and I'm a married man."

"Not happily, I can call bullshit when I hear it, just tell me the truth you're not leaving your wife, I am grown I can handle the truth."

"Ashaunti if you could handle the truth you would not be asking me these questions. You have allowed your feelings to overwhelm you, I have been married to my wife for twenty-five years, I'm not leaving my wife, and I would advise you not to leave your husband." He cleared his throat.

"Okay well that settles it, twenty-five hundred via PayPal, Thank you." I announced full of nasty attitude.

"What is that for Ashaunti?" He asked with his eyebrows raised.

"My pain and suffering." I grabbed my coat, my bag, and left the hotel room.

By the time I entered the parking lot, I had already received a notification to my PayPal account. All I could do was laugh, Doc didn't want to lose this pussy and I didn't want to lose my allowance.

Nila

2 weeks later

Regardless of what anybody thinks, I love

being at school and away from home with my

parents and their bad energy. The constant

arguing it's mainly my mom, but still they act

like it doesn't affect everybody there. My mom

will start the argument, normally daddy never

argues back with her and whenever she's done

she leaves. It's been a pattern for at least the

last six months, maybe even a year, being in an

unhappy household is hell. There is no other

place I would rather be than school. Plus, I can

see my boyfriend Braxton and my bestie

KeAnna.

I was sitting inside of my third period class in

a daze, I didn't even notice the teacher calling

my name.

"Nila, Mrs. Downs is calling on you." KeAnna

tapped on my shoulder.

"Ma'am?"

"Nila do you have your homework assignments from Monday night? There is no grade for you in the student portal." Mrs. Downs was looking at her computer.

KeAnna tapped me on my side again with some papers, my girl was a life saver because I hadn't completed the homework.

"Che, Che, Cheeeeater." I looked over at Braxton and Niko Jr. trying to get me caught, hating asses.

"Yes Ma'am, I have it." I walked up to Mrs. Downs desk area.

On my way back to my desk I looked at Braxton and Niko Jr. seating in the back laughing. Braxton was shaking his head and when I read his lips, he was saying damn shame, I smiled and stuck out my tongue. Him and Niko Jr. both need to mind their own business, what they worried about my work for? The bell rung and Mrs. Downs dismissed the class.

I could not get out of the class well enough before I saw Ms. Labo waiting there now, I know I can't be in any trouble.

"Hi Nila, how has everything been going with class and turn in assignments?"

"Dang friend what you did now?" KeAnna asked.

"She has not done anything KeAnna, I'm only checking on her and I wanted to ask her something if that is okay, Nila does your dad have a mechanic shop? I meant to ask you the other day."

"Yes Ma'am, Webb Mechanics off of Sherwood Forest." I answered.

"I thought I recognized him, I get my vehicle serviced there sometimes, he does a great job."

"Yup."

"Well you ladies hurry and get to your next class and have a good day."

"Yes ma'am." Me and KeAnna both responded.

Ashaunti

I walked into the office after being off a few

days, having a long night, and little to no sleep

at all, I'm not feeling this work day today. But

duties call and I'm the man of the house, after I

brewed a pot of hot coffee, I turned on my

desktop to see how many appointments we

had here for today. Between the paperwork

that I needed to complete, and my feelings all over the place, I could not concentrate. I only saw Doc once and I was hoping not to see him anymore because once he is in my sight, the more in my feelings I become.

"Good morning Ashaunti!" My medical assistant Moni walked into the office happy as hell.

"Good Morning Moni, even though I don't consider this to be a good morning, I should have said bad morning, that makes more sense." I got up to pour me a cup of coffee.

When I finished I sat back for a moment not saying anything else just thinking when Moni interrupted my thoughts.

"Ashaunti!"

"What's up?"

"Are you okay? Look like you are focusing hard as hell."

"I'm okay, I am thinking."

"Thinking about who Doctor Fitzgerald Pelhan? Ashaunti you better let that go before it messier than you can handle."

"Moni what are you talking about?"

"I'm talking about you falling in love with our boss who is a married man!"

"Listen Moni."

"No Ashaunti, you listen!" She cut me off.

"You haven't had enough yet?" She raised

her eyebrows.

"Enough of what?" I was playing dumb.

"Let me speak to you in a language you can

understand. How long are you going to be

sticking that married man dick down your

throat?"

"However long he is going to put his married

tongue on my kitty."

Moni was sitting there shaking her head,

well she asked and I told her.

"Why do women like you make it bad for the good women like me that deserves a good man?"

"How the hell do I make it bad, what the hell does that mean?"

"It means you have a good man at home, and you are still out here searching for something instead of making your own marriage work." Moni said now filing her paperwork.

"Moni how do you know Niko is a good man?"

"Even if your husband isn't a good man, you make women look bad by knowingly sleeping with another woman's husband. When I see

you messing up, I'm going to tell you, and I

don't care how you feel."

"Moni just please mind the business that

pays you!" I laughed and sipped from my

coffee.

"The truth hurts."She said.

Our conversation had gotten so deep we

didn't even notice someone had approached

the desk.

"May I help you?" Moni asked.

"Yes, I'm here to see Dr. Fitzgerald." The

lady asked.

"Is he expecting you Ma'am?"

"He is not expecting me."

"Good Morning ladies, hey baby what are you doing here? Doc walked up and greeted all of us.

"I am here to bring you to breakfast, maybe get a smoothie is that okay?" The lady said.

"Yes, let me finish up a few things first, come sit inside of my office." Doc motioned for his wife to follow him.

As soon as the coast was clear Moni started again.

"Oooooh, so that's wifey huh? Damn shame she does not know how much of a whore her husband is."

"Yup that is his wife Jessika, her pictures are all over his office."

"I don't pay attention to all of that, but I am glad to know that you do because that further tells me you should know better."

"Whatever Moni." I stood up and walked off.

I am an adult and I know right from wrong, and what I'm doing is wrong no way around it. I have no business dealing with Doc, he is my boss, he is married, and I am married however, it's done now and I can't take it back.

Niko

Some of the words Ashaunti uses when she

speaks to me cut likes a knife, She says some of

the things so much I think she really feels that

way. What happened to us being happily ever

after, I can't pinpoint where our marriage went

sour, but the frequent disagreements are

starting to take a toll on me. Ashaunti

sometimes goes out of the way to make it

appear that I'm the reason everything is falling

apart. When I come home in the evenings, she

rushes out of the bedroom, and to the living

room, where she balls up on the couch in her

damn phone all night. Now truth be told I never

claimed to be a perfect husband, but damn at

least give me the credit for trying. It doesn't

matter how hard I try to help my marriage or

my family, it won't work without the effort

from everyone. Lately, I've been staying at the

shop because it seems to be the only place

where I'm not unhappy. Working on my

motorbike and my customer's cars are my

special therapy, maybe it will keep Ashaunti

happy too. My mama always said if someone

isn't happy with you then nine times out of ten,

they are happy somewhere else I don't know

what my wife problem is..

My day at the shop was complete, but the

last place I wanted to go to, was the home I

shared with my bipolar wife and out of order

children. Although I didn't want to go there, I

know I had to because Ashaunti can't handle

both Nila and Niko Jr by herself. She has been

allowing too much shit fly with them anyway,

it's time to get some order around there, I will

try to anyway. On my way to the house, I

stopped and picked up some Popeyes chicken,

I'm sure Ashaunti either is not home or did not

cook. When I drove up to the driveway and saw

Niko Jr. sitting on the side of the house

smoking, I figured the changes around here will

start with him, but I'm going to hit that blunt

first.

Nila

I was inside of my bedroom being a mute,,

glaring out of the window, the rain was lightly

falling and I use it to clear my mind. My parents

have not been around each other lately, so the

house has been silent with no arguing. That is

great because I've had enough headaches, my

phone notifications went off and it was

KeAnna.

KeAnna: Hey Bestie, wyd?

Me: About to do so home work.

KeAnna: Did you tell your mom?

Me: Not yet.

KeAnna: I'm outside of your house

Me: Ring the doorbell, someone will answer.

Me and my mother don't have a close relationship, therefore I know it will not be easy telling her that I'm pregnant in high school. I repeated my parent's cycle and I'm more fearful of breaking my daddy's heart.

"Nila, KeAnna is here!" My mother yelled from the living room.

"Tell her to come to my room," I yelled back

KeAnna and Niko Jr. must have had some

plans today, that is the only way KeAnna would

come over last minute and she never

mentioned coming over last night.

"Hey, Nila!" KeAnna came into my bedroom

all full of life.

"Hey, girl."

"Dang, why are you so dry today, is Niko

here?"

"KeAnna you know Niko home, that's what

you came here." I rolled my eyes and started

folding my laundry.

"Salty much, I sure did!"

I already knew what was up with KeAnna, it's our normal routine. At my parents' house my bedroom and Niko Jr. bedroom were connected by a bathroom that we shared. KeAnna slid the door over and went to Niko's room, we always left both sliding doors opened just in case. This is the same routine I use whenever Braxton comes over, he would front like he was visiting Niko Jr, but we all knew what the play was.

Jessika

Ashaunti thought she would walk into this hotel room to my husband, not this time honey, when she seen me, you would have thought she seen a ghost.

"The gig is up honey, you thought you would come in here and fuck my husband for an allowance again huh? No ma'am not today, I have allowed Fitzgerald to have more than enough fun it is my turn now. I would say you have ruined my marriage, but you didn't the damage was already done. Let me explain something to you, I have twenty-five years of

marriage and if anything was to happen to

Fitzgerald, my low-down dirty husband, it all

goes to me, his wife! Every copper penny and

silver dime of it, Ashaunti you aren't Fitzgerald

first sidepiece honey, and probably won't be

the last. I'm married to my money and you're

starting to touch that, we have a problem. I

have played Fitzgerald game long enough it's

my turn to have some fun.

If you want my tender dick husband, you go

right ahead honey however, there will be no

more income attached to him I can promise

you that. Fitzgerald falls in love with every

piece of outside cat he sticks his dick inside of,

so don't feel special honey."

"He is leaving you, ask him!" Ashaunti said.

"Oh you're bold, you pick up your got damn

phone and ask him where the hell he's going?

Since you have it made up in your mind and

you know so much, you ask him! I yelled."

"No need to cause a scene you have gotten

your point across crystal clear."Ashaunti

started.

"If I didn't have nothing to lose, I would let

you have it. However, I have everything to lose,

I built that man from the ground up that is my

work honey. My accounts are well, and enough,

my home was built from the ground up, I can

retire, and I have never had a job, you know

why? Because honey I was smart, every

business my husband puts his hands on I am

tied into it, every investment has my name is

attached to it. My children college funding is

zeroed out, my insurance policies are also well.

I am good honey Fitzgerald is not hurting me he

is only hurting himself." I grabbed my purse,

walked passed her, and out of the room.

Simernecia Shena

Ashaunti

When I opened the door to that hotel room and saw Jessika sitting there, I was shocked. My first thought was to run out of that room, why would she come there? She set me up, Jessika was the one texting me to meet her there, she knew me and Docs entire routine. My situation with Doc was over when he made it clear that we would be nothing more. I know Doc loves his wife and our relationship was only a convenient at work affair, but when you get

some attention you can't get at home, you

start catching feelings. My grandfather is

probably turning in his grave over my choices

and actions lately, my mother defends me

through everything but, she will not defend a

martial affair. Mainly because she has

experienced many affairs with my father, that

man has outside children everywhere.

Today is my day to pick up the twins from

school and guess who is nowhere in sight? That

damn Nila. I love my daughter, but she is doing

too much these days. Niko Jr came to the car

and soon as he opened my car door the smell

of marijuana almost knocked me out of the driver seat.

"Hey Ma!" He said all cheerful.

"Where is your sister and why do you smell like that boy?"

"She left with her boyfriend and because I was cutting grass."

"Get your lying ass out of my car, get out lying ass!" I fussed at Niko Jr.

This boy must be out of his mind, he can walk his ass home since he wants to be grown, and I pulled off.

Simernecia Shena

Jessika

My husband is a very attractive man so I can see women wanting a sample of him and he has money so that's a double win. Fitzgerald five feet nine, slim-medium build, with a light complexion, and doesn't age not one bit.

I know who Ashaunti is now and I also know about her ongoing affair with my husband. His affairs have never bothered me much until recently, he has become too sloppy and the money that is transferred to accounts is not going to keep happening. Everything that I have going on Fitzgerald funds it, from my business, to my monthly vacations paid for. Now, if he continues giving her benefits, that will cut into myself and my children expenses, I will not allow that.

Ashaunti sleeps with my husband frequently, whenever I'm away on vacation business or leisure, Fitzgerald uses her up for sex and she is so weak, she allows it. I called my sister because my sister Ming has always been my go-to for everything.

"Hello Jess!" She answered.

"Hey Ming, how are you?"

"All is well, what do you have going on?"

"Other than the fact that my husband is up to his old tricks, Fitzgerald can find any time to cheat that man is sick Ming."

"Oh my gosh Jessika not again, he was doing so well."

"Yeah well he has relapsed, I'm one hundred percent sure he is having an affair with the nurse at his office Ashaunti Webb, how about that for convenience."

"Did you say Ashaunti Webb! Jessika, I know her, her kids go to my school, and her husband often services my car."

"Oh really, Ming I think she needs to be taught a lesson, do you think her husband is attractive? You have been needing a man." I said to Ming.

"First off, mind your business, and Jessika you are too old to play get back. Jessika just leave well enough alone because I know you're not insinuating I attempt to fool with her husband." Ming responded.

"Ming would you do that, fool around with that man?" I wondered.

"No I have class about myself, what the hell has gotten into you?"

"You're right Ming I'm sorry! Look I'm going to call you a little later my husband is home."

I hung up with Ming and started with Fitzgerald soon as he walked through the door.

"Hey Jessika, how was your day?" He asked strolling into the master bedroom.

"My day was great, just wasn't as busy as your day Doctor."

"Yeah honey I have had a very tedious day at the office."

"And is that it?"

"Jessika why are you standing there looking like that?"

"Let's just say I know what is going on and like I assured you the last time, there would be no more hurting and no more tears. You my dear shall pay for all the damage you have caused."

"Jessika please do not start being delusional."

"Funny that's what every man says when he knows his significant other has him, dead ass spot on. Nonetheless, I made certain to cross my I's and dot my T's this time." I announced.

"Jessika what is going on now?" Fitzgerald asked as he yawned.

"What is going on is my husband is still out here chasing women and spending big bucks while he's at it, I know everything and I met your little sex slave Ashaunti today."

He stood there with guilt written on his face.

"What?"

"You heard exactly what I said Fitzgerald, so please don't play the fool now. I have played your fool for so many years, but those days are over."

"I would tell you to fire her and make a complete uproar over everything, but what sense would that make? You're still going to do

whatever you want to do regardless. The only

difference now is, I'm going to do whatever it is

I want, with whoever I want, and at your

expense. You wanted an open marriage and

now you have one, let the fun begin."

Ashaunti

Today was a day for spring cleaning and I'm starting with the twin's bathroom, but before I got the chance to bleach everything down, I received an incoming call.

"Hello."

"Hello, Mrs. Webb this is the nurse from Charter High School and I have Nila here in the clinic with me saying she is not feeling well today."

"Okay, may I speak with her?"

"Ma'am?" Nila answered the phone.

"Hey what is going with you? Nila you are starting to miss too many days, you better pray this does not affect your grades."

"Yes ma'am."

We disconnected the call and on my way out of the bathroom, the pregnancy in the trash caught me off guard. Oh my God and it's positive, that's why she's so sick, why in the hell would my child do that, this cycle cannot repeat itself. Nila can't take care of a baby and

Niko is going to have fit, how did I not pay

attention to my child? My life is all over the

place, I have had an affair on my husband,

created an unhappy marriage, inattentive to

my children, and I broke the promises I'd given

my grandfather. How did I allow my selfishness

to take over me and let my family down? I

hurried grabbed my keys and was in route to

the twin's school to pick up Nila.

On the ride to the school I imagine what I

would say when I seen on my daughter. That

moment soon came Nila was sitting in the

office looking like a little girl, I walked in and

gave Nila the biggest hug. I could have cussed

and fussed, but my child does not have an idea, what it is going to be like being a teen mother.

"Hi, I'm here to check her out." I said to the secretary.

"Just sign the paper on the counter and she is dismissed for the day."

When we made it back to the car, I had to take a deep breath before I could speak.

"Nila, how many times have we spoke about unprotected sex and teen pregnancies?"

"A lot." She replied looking confused.

"Well what happened? You were not safe if you're pregnant!"

"How do you know mom?"

"Nila! How long were you going to hide your pregnancy from me and your father?"

"Until it was time for me to have the baby." She replied and the look on her face showed me how honest she was being.

"Do you even know how far along you are? Have you seen an OBGYN? You have to tell your dad he's going to flip out."

"Four months along and can you tell daddy please?"

"Four mouths, why did you just take a pregnancy test? No Nila you can tell your father." I started my car.

"I did not just take a pregnancy test I took

one months ago at the youth outreach center."

"Why was there a positive pregnancy test in

your bathroom?"

"I don't know I never took a test at home."

She answered.

"Nila, I know the test isn't for Niko Jr." I spat.

"I don't have anything to do with that."

Ashaunti

The ride to the mechanic shop was never a

long ride, even when I was younger, I would

walk there to see my grandfather. It was a

quick walk or ride on the bicycle because we

didn't live that far. When I turned into the

parking lot to the shop everything looks

different, it looks so nice! I haven't been here

in so long, I didn't how much Niko had upgraded this place. The building had been repainted, brand new signs, new doors, it looks so bright, and ready for business. My grandfather would be so pleased at how nicely Niko invested in this place.

Instead of me going inside, I sat there and admired how beautiful the shop is now, I also rehearsed what I wanted to say to my husband. Just as I was about to exit my car, everything I wanted to say I forgot, I watched Niko walking out of Webb's Mechanic Shop smiling like he had just experienced the time of his life. My husband has not smiled like this in forever and I didn't waste any time getting out of my car

rushing towards him.

"Niko what the hell is going on here, who is

she?" I asked approaching my husband and the

very attractive female.

"What is the problem Ashaunti and why are

you here?" He stood there with a settled look

on his face.

"You tell me what the problem is Niko and

what do you mean why am I here? Because I

can be here that's why!" I glanced at the lady

one more time and I could not help, but to ask

her. "Excuse me are you the counselor from my

kid's school? Why are here? Are you sleeping

with my husband?" I asked the lady.

"Really Ashaunti? This is what we're doing

now? This is not the time or the place this is my

job, we will talk later."

"No Niko I want to know now, are you

fucking this lady? Is this lady the reason you're

smiling and always at this damn shop?"

"Ashaunti, I'm not going to allow you to

disrespect yourself or her. This is Ms. Ming

Labo, yes she is the counselor at the high

school, she is also a financial advisor that has

helped me take out some loans and discover

some credit to upgrade this shop over the past several weeks." Niko explained.

"Can you call me when my vehicle is finished Webb?"

"Make sure I'm around when she picks up her car, Webb!" I said sarcastically.

She rolled her eyes and went to a car that was waiting, when she opened the door, I noticed the driver was Jessika, Doc's wife. What type of games is this bitch playing? The pair slowing pulled off.

"Ashaunti, why are you acting an ass while I'm at work? Look I'll come to your house to talk to you when my work day is over. As you can now see I do work, I made an investment

into myself, this company, and twenty-five

thousand for each of the kids college funding."

"My house? My house? You are a married

man Niko Webb, that is our house!"

"You are funny Ashaunti, now it's our house

because you think I'm out here doing to you

dirty like you're doing to me. You're out here

living how you want and doing what you want,

like you don't have a husband or children.

You're always gone and when you are home,

you are sitting somewhere smiling inside of

your phone. I don't know what you have going

on Ashaunti and I'm not the type of man to go

digging trying to find out shit, you know that. I

could do the same shit and not give a fuck;

however, I am a better man than that. If

something is going sour on your end and God

wants me to see it, he will reveal it sooner or

later."

My husband left me standing there and

went back into his shop, I rushed to my car and

was in my route home I could not help but

think how badly I had messed up. My husband

was all the man I needed him to be and would

never do the things to me that I have done to

him. Niko built his brand, his company, and

upgraded, while I was nowhere around to

support him. I want to fix this, fix my marriage,

my children, just everything overall.

Niko

Finally closing the shop for the day, I covered my bike and headed home, when drove up my driveway I could see almost every light on the inside of the house. But when I did make it inside, I was hit by the smell of a meal being prepared and it took me by surprise.

"Damn it smells good in here." I said aloud.

The house was cleaned Anita Baker was playing in the background Ashaunti only listens to Anita Baker when she's in a good mood. I went into the kitchen to grab a drink Ashaunti was standing there in a nice little two-piece Nike shorts set. My dick was hard, but I wasn't about to try nothing because we never have sex when we are not on the same page. It's been that way for a while, and I've been sexless for a while too.

"What's up Ashaunti, where is Niko Jr and Nila?"

"They are around here somewhere are you hungry?" She asked.

"Now I'm not trying to start nothing, but you're offering me a meal, you trying to kill me?" I laughed, but I was serious.

"Kill you for what, I'm just trying to do better if that is okay with you?" She explained.

"I'll get something later, I want to speak to the kids now, you said they both need to tell me something, what is going on around here? All of you are tripping."

"Before you talk to them you should eat something." Ashaunti insisted.

"Fix me a little something and call those kids in here, never mind I'll call them. Nila! Niko!" I yelled.

Niko Jr. was the first to enter the area where

I was, he was almost as tall as I was.

"Sir?"

"You need to tell your dad what you have

going on Niko." Ashaunti said.

Nila was now standing there behind her

brother.

"What's up Da?"

"Boy don't what's up Da me! What's going

on son, talk to me?"

"Ummm."

"I'll start." Nila cut him off.

My baby girl stood there and look me directly in my eyes with her eyes filled with tears.

"Daddy, I'm pregnant."

I threw my hands on my face I was in disbelief to what I was hearing.

"Pregnant? Not my baby girl."

I looked over at Ashaunti who was shaking her head acknowledging it was true. I didn't know how to respond only thing I felt was hurt.

"Alright Niko what's up?" I asked my son.

"I ain't pregnant Da."

"Shit I know that boy, stop playing!"

"KeAnna is though."

Deja fucking Vu!

"Man are you two serious? Both of you are out her having sex, you shouldn't be, and then you weren't practicing safe sex. Man, I can't believe history is about to repeat itself two times, what the hell." I threw my hands behind my head.

I got up from the dinner table and went outside, this was too much to handle. Feeling like I have failed my children, I don't know where to go from here. Unaware of where I went wrong with those children, I know I wasn't perfect, but never did I expect this. Both of my children are about to have babies in high school, what's done is done I just have to

support my kids, make sure they get through

this last year of school, and prepare them for

what's coming. So far as my marriage that is

still unclear despite everything that's going on

my family needs me and I will try anything to

make it work. That is the promise that I made,

It is too many broken families and I promised to

keep mine together.

I walked over to my truck, where a text from

Ming Labo came through.

Ming: Hi!

Me: Hey your car will be ready tomorrow.

Ming: Okay, cool deal.

Me: Webb, your wife insulted me by asking were we sleeping together that was rude and absurd. However, maybe she did it out of her own guilt about having an affair with my brother in law, her boss.

Enjoyed this short story? Hate to see it end?
Stay on the lookout for, Princess of the Trap Releasing May 2019

Follow me on social media

Facebook @ Shena Simernecia

Instagram @_author_simerneciashena

CPSIA information can be obtained
at www.ICGtesting.com
Printed in the USA
LVHW021740270619
622554LV00015B/551